KU-496-716

A Note to Parents and Teachers

SAINSBURY'S READING SCHEME is a compelling reading programme for children, designed in conjunction with leading literacy experts.

Action-packed, engaging, easy-to-read stories are complemented by vibrant illustrations to fire the imaginations of new readers. Each book in the **SAINSBURY'S READING SCHEME** is guaranteed to capture a child's interest while developing his or her reading skills, general knowledge and love of reading.

The five levels of the programme are aimed at different reading abilities, enabling you to choose the books that are exactly right for your child.

Yellow Level – Learning to read
Green Level – Beginning to read
Gold Level – Beginning to read alone
Ruby Level – Reading alone
Sapphire Level – Proficient readers

The "normal" age at which a child begins to read can be anywhere from three to eight years old, so these levels are only a general guideline.

No matter which level you select, you can be sure that you're helping children learn to read, then read to learn!

To Isla and Ewan

First published in Great Britain by HarperCollins *Children's Books* in 2007
as a story in *Wizzbang Wizard: Dragon Danger and Grasshopper Glue*
This edition published in partnership with Sainsbury's Reading Scheme in 2014
HarperCollins *Children's Books* is a division of HarperCollins*Publishers* Ltd,
77-85 Fulham Palace Road, Hammersmith, London W6 8JB

Visit us on the web at
www.harpercollins.co.uk

1 3 5 7 9 10 8 6 4 2

Dragon Danger
Text © 2007 Scoular Anderson
Illustrations © 2007 and 2014 Scoular Anderson

ISBN 978-0-00-759507-5

Printed and bound in China

Conditions of Sale
This book is sold subject to the condition that it shall not, by way of trade
or otherwise, be lent, re-sold, hired out or otherwise circulated without the
publisher's prior written consent in any form of binding or cover other than
that in which it is published and without a similar condition including this
condition being imposed on the subsequent purchaser.

Sainsbury's
Reading Scheme

Sapphire Level
Proficient readers

Dragon Danger

Scoular Anderson

HarperCollins *Children's Books*

Chapter One

Near the little village of Muddling, at the very end of Lumpy Lane, was a very strange house. Sometimes there were spots on the roof and sometimes there were stripes. Sometimes the walls were green and sometimes they changed to blue. For this was a wizard's house and it was a magical place to live.

The wizard was in the wizard room where all the magic books and potions were kept. He was a young wizard called Freddy Frogpurse and he was sitting on the edge of the table, dangling his legs.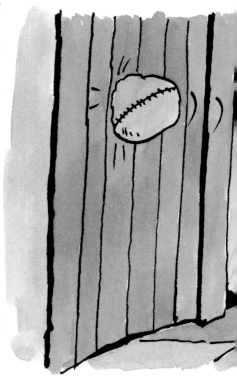

"Now!" Freddy shouted.

At that moment, a leather ball stuffed with feathers dropped down in front of Freddy from the ceiling. With a skilful flick of his foot, he sent the ball whizzing across the room. It hit the middle of the door with a loud

whump!

"GOAL!" shouted Freddy. "That's fifteen goals and only two misses so far!"

 The ball slowly floated up from the floor to the ceiling. It drifted across the room towards Freddy then stopped just above his head.

"Now!" Freddy shouted again.

The ball dropped. Freddy kicked. The ball shot towards the door, but this time the door opened suddenly. There was a thump, a squeak and a cloud of black smoke.

Freddy leapt off the table.

"Odds! Are you hurt?"

He bent down and lifted the ball from the floor. Underneath was a small dragon.

Freddy carefully picked up the little creature.

"I'm really sorry, Odds!" said Freddy. "I was just—"

The dragon struggled free. He rattled his scales angrily and blew another puff of black smoke through his nostrils.

"Master Freddy!" said the dragon. "This is not the proper behaviour for a wizard!"

The dragon was called Odds-and-Ends and he was the house dragon of

Wizard Cottage. The cottage belonged to a very grand wizard called Doctor Sneezer Frogpurse.

He had gone off on a World Wide Wizard Walk and had left his great nephew Freddy to look after his house.

"Master Freddy!" snapped the little dragon. "May I remind you that you are supposed to be learning about magic so you can become a clever wizard like your Great Uncle!"

Freddy pointed to the leather ball.

"Don't you think the spell I put on my football was clever?" he said. "It means I can practise when it's wet outside."

"That's not proper magic," snapped the dragon. "That's just silly nonsense. I think you ought to get back to your books, Master Freddy."

Freddy heaved a sigh. "You're right, Odds." He turned and went to the bookshelves, which stretched right up to the ceiling. He pulled a huge book from a shelf and laid it

on the table.

"That's better," said Odds-and-Ends. He turned and flew out of the room, blowing one last, angry smoke ring.

I wonder why he's in such a bad mood? Freddy thought. *Now where was I?*

He opened the big book and flicked through it. It was *Volume One* of the *Wizard's Handbook* (Fifty Volumes), but Freddy hadn't got any further than the first few pages.

"Part 4: Stretching and shrinking

spells," Freddy read. Then he gave a little yawn. "This first bit seems quite easy."

He picked up his wand, gave it a few practice twirls, then cast a spell.

"Wizzbang-a-thingumajig! stretch-stretch-really-big!"

he chanted and pointed his wand at the curtains.

The curtains began to stretch longer and longer. They piled up on the floor in huge folds. Soon, they filled half the room and headed towards Freddy like waves.

Freddy grabbed the *Wizard's Handbook* from the table and flicked through the pages again. He found a spell just in time.

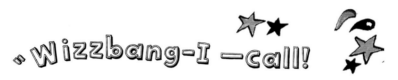

"Wizzbang-I —call! Shrink-really-small!"

The waves of curtain stopped growing and began to retreat.

"Phew!" said Freddy.

But now the curtains were the size of hankies, dangling from the curtain rail.

Just then, Freddy heard a shout from outside.

"Freddy! Are you in there? Have you got the football?"

It was Freddy's pal, Cubby. *There won't be any harm in having a quick kick-about with my friends,* Freddy thought. After checking that Odds-and-Ends wasn't lurking in the house, he tucked the football under his arm and went out to join his friends.

Chapter Two

Freddy tiptoed back into the house after the football game. He was sure he'd get a telling-off from Odds-and-Ends, but the dragon didn't seem to be around. Freddy looked in all the rooms of Wizard

Cottage and in the garden shed, but Odds-and-Ends was not to be found. By bedtime the little dragon had still not appeared.

"That's very, very strange," muttered Freddy, as he went up the stairs to bed.

In the morning, there was still no sign of him.

I'll go down to the village and ask if anyone has seen him there, thought Freddy, so after breakfast he set out down Lumpy Lane towards Muddling.

Mr Green the blacksmith was hammering away at a horseshoe in his smithy. **BLAM! BLAM! BLAM!**

"Have— **BLAM!** you— **BLAM!**
seen— **BLAM!** my— **BLAM!**
house— **BLAM!** dragon— **BLAM!**

Mr— **BLAM!** Green—?" asked Freddy between hammer blows.

"Lost your dragon?" said Mr Green, as he stopped to wipe the sweat off his face. He gave Freddy a crooked smile with his one crooked tooth. "I reckon you will have to be looking for a new one then. They're touchy things these dragons. I wouldn't trust one as far as I could throw one. Give me a horse with four good feet firmly on the ground!" and he went back to his hammering. **BLAM! BLAM! BLAM!**

Now Freddy felt really unhappy. Perhaps Odds-and-Ends had flown away to find some other young wizard who was keen on reading books and learning spells. Perhaps the little dragon was not to be trusted.

What am I going to tell Uncle Sneezer? thought Freddy, as he walked on. *How am I going to explain that he needs a new house dragon? Besides, I'll miss him. Wizard Cottage won't be the same without Odds, even if he does tell me off too much.*

Freddy found himself standing across the road from Mrs Muncher's cake stall. He glanced

across at all the piles of delicious cakes, biscuits and scones.

A cake would cheer me up a lot, he thought and so he crossed the road.

"You look a bit down-in-the-mouth

this morning, Master Freddy," said Mrs Muncher cheerily.

"It's because Odds-and-Ends has disappeared," wailed Freddy. "I haven't seen him since midday yesterday. I think he's flown away and will never come back."

"Oh, Master Freddy," said Mrs Muncher. "I've never heard of a dragon deserting its house. It will be Odds-and-Ends' birthday."

"Did you say his *birthday*?" said Freddy.

"Oh yes. Dragons always disappear for a little while on their birthday, you know," Mrs Muncher went on. "Of course,

they live for a very long time and only have a birthday every ten years. I remember the day your Great Uncle Sneezer got Odds-and-Ends. He was such a sweet little pup! He was about seventy years old, but that's very young for a dragon. Your Great Uncle—"

"But why do they disappear on their birthday?" asked Freddy impatiently.

"They go off to shed their scales, my dear," said Mrs Muncher. "They go off to a quiet place every ten years, shed their old scales and grow nice, shiny new ones. It takes a little while and makes them very grumpy. I think the new scales are quite itchy and—"

"Thank you, Mrs Muncher," said Freddy, as a broad grin spread across his face. "You've really cheered me up! I thought Odds-and-Ends had run away for good!"

"Oh, I'm sure he hasn't, my dear," said Mrs Muncher.

"Perhaps I ought to buy Odds-and-Ends a birthday cake," said Freddy eagerly.

"I don't think dragons eat cake, my love," said Mrs Muncher. "All they seem to eat is that dragon weed, which grows down by the river. And honey. They're partial to a little bit of honey. Why not go and ask Mr Buzzwell the beekeeper for some honey? I'm sure he'd—"

"Thanks, Mrs Muncher!" said Freddy. "I'll go and do that!"

"Before you go, love, here's a little something to keep you cheery!" said Mrs Muncher and she handed Freddy a strawberry tart.

Freddy thanked Mrs Muncher again and headed for home, nibbling his strawberry tart.

He called in on Mr Buzzwell on the way.

"I'd like a jar of honey for my house dragon, please, Mr Buzzwell!" Freddy shouted from a distance, since Mr Buzzwell was standing surrounded by beehives and angry bees.

Mr Buzzwell came across to Freddy.

"I'm sorry, Freddy, I have no jars of honey just at the moment," he said. He saw the smile fall from Freddy's face. "I tell you what! I have an extra little

beehive down in my field. How about I
let you have the hive and your dragon
can help himself to honey?"

"That would be really kind of you, Mr

Buzzwell," said Freddy, cheering up again.

"I'll wait till evening," said Mr Buswell. "All the bees will be inside for the night and I'll bring the hive to you then."

Freddy thanked Mr Buzzwell again

then ran down to the river. He picked an armful of dragon weed. It was very prickly and had a nasty smell.

"I don't know how Odds-and-Ends can eat this stuff," said Freddy, as he tried

to carry the pile of weed home and hold his nose at the same time. He dumped the weed on the table and rolled up his sleeves.

"Now, how on earth do I turn this into a birthday cake?" he said.

chapter Three

Freddy boiled the dragon weed for quite a long time and it filled the kitchen with its awful smell. When it had cooled, he emptied it out of the pot on to a plate. He covered it in green icing to match Odds-

and-Ends' scales and stuck a candle on top.

It didn't look much like a cake, more like a lumpy pillow. The candle kept toppling over on its side. Freddy stood and looked at the cake for a while.

"It's not a very pretty cake to give to Odds," he said to himself. "I wonder how I could improve it?"

He marched thoughtfully round and round the kitchen until a good idea popped into his head.

"I've got it! I could give the cake wings and it could fly out to meet Odds as he came home! That would be a nice surprise!"

Freddy ran through to the wizard room. His heart sank as he looked at the rows of books on magic which stretched from floor to ceiling.

"If I had done my homework, I'd know what I was looking for," he sighed.

He looked at the titles of the books nearest him.

1001 Dandelion Potions

Fun with Festoons

Toothache Treatment by Magic

Everything You Want to Know about Dragons

Help with Hurricanes

Flying - Fast or Far?

"Aha!" said Freddy with delight. "This sounds just what I'm looking for!"

He pulled *Flying - Fast or Far?* from the shelf and opened it on the table.

As he flicked through the pages, he stopped smiling.

"I don't understand any of this," he muttered. "Flying spells are more difficult than I thought."

He was just about to close the book when he caught sight of something on the back page.

If all else fails, try this simple spell for a short flight...

Freddy threw the book down, picked up his wand and dashed back to the kitchen.

He pointed at the cake with his wand, gave it a little twirl and said...

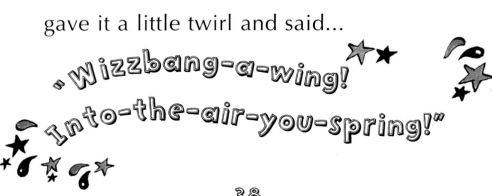

"Wizzbang-a-wing! Into-the-air-you-spring!"

The cake gave a little twitch then shot into the air. However, the spell wasn't quite right. The cake only had *one* wing so it flew round in wobbly circles, bumping into things.

"I've got to sort this out!" said Freddy. "Odds could return at any moment."

He chased the cake round the kitchen, casting the spell again and again but each time he pointed his wand, the cake lurched out of the way. That meant the spell landed on something else. Soon, the dishcloth was fluttering round the kitchen, too, along with the frying pan and the kettle. Next, a whole pile of plates took to the air.

Just at that moment, Odds-and-Ends darted through the open window. There was a splosh, a squeak and a puff of black smoke as the dragon collided with his flying birthday cake.

"Master Freddy!" snapped the little dragon, as he dodged a flock of forks. "Will you please behave!"

"I'm really sorry, Odds!" cried Freddy in horror.

Odds-and-Ends fluttered down to the table and wiped some of the icing from his eyes with his little paws.

"I was just trying to make a birthday cake," said Freddy.

"*Birthday?*" squeaked the dragon. "Whose birthday?"

"Why... er... yours," said Freddy.

"It's not *my* birthday," said the dragon. "It's not my birthday for another seven years."

"Mrs Muncher told me it was your

birthday," said Freddy. "She said you got new scales on your birthday and that was why you were grumpy."

"Oh, Master Freddy," said Odds-and-Ends with a sigh. "I'm sorry if I have sounded a bit tetchy. It's nothing to do with my scales. It's because of Dragon Ormudd."

"Who's that?" asked Freddy.

"He's a fat, ugly dragon and if you see him, it means trouble," said Odds-and-Ends.

"And have you seen him, Odds?" asked Freddy.

"I need cleaning up, before I answer that," said the little dragon, looking at the birthday cake on his scales.

Freddy pulled a big pot into the middle of the floor and filled it with water. He lifted the dragon from the table, put him into the pot and began to wash the cake and icing from his scales with a

scrubbing brush. It wasn't easy, as Freddy had to dodge the black smoke and sparks which Odds-and-Ends always puffed out when he was angry.

When the dragon was clean, Freddy lifted him out of the pot. Odds-and-Ends gave himself such a big shake, his scales rattled. He flew round the kitchen twice to dry off his wings then he landed back on the table.

"I have seen Dragon Ormudd," he said. "I have been following him around, watching what he's up to. He is nearby and that means trouble because he likes to raid wizards' houses."

"Oh!" squeaked Freddy, and the scrubbing brush dropped out of his hand on to the floor with a clunk. "Is that... er... dangerous?"

"It's dangerous and unpleasant," said

Odds-and-Ends. "He'll burst in and gobble up all the bottles in the wizard room before you know what's happened. A dragon  with a belly full of magic potions is not a dragon you want to be near."

Freddy felt a cold shiver run from the top of his head right down to his little toes.

"However," said Odds-and-Ends, "it is a house dragon's job to protect his wizard's house as best he can. So, Master Freddy, I want you to promise that, whatever happens tonight, you will stay in bed."

"Yes... er... if you say so," said Freddy, feeling a bit puzzled.

"Whatever you hear, whatever you feel, whatever you see, you must *not*

look out of the window *or* leave your bedroom," said the dragon. "Do I make myself clear?"

"Yes, Odds," said Freddy.

"I will be ready and waiting if Dragon Ormudd comes," said Odds-and-Ends. "He will not enter Wizard Cottage as long as I'm around!"

And with that he flew out of the door.

Chapter Four

Freddy went to bed that night and tossed and turned in his sleep. He woke up several times and each time he stretched out a hand and pulled a lever on the clock. This was one of Great Uncle Sneezer's favourite magical inventions – a speaking clock, which not only told the time but told the weather, too.

"The time is fifteen minutes to midnight. The weather is cool and clear..."

"The time is twenty minutes past midnight. The weather is cool and clear..."

"The time is twenty-five minutes to one in the morning. The weather is cool and clear..."

After the last time-check, Freddy sat up

in bed. He was sure he could hear a noise in the garden, but he remembered that Odds-and-Ends had warned him not to look outside.

I'm sure a quick peep wouldn't do any harm, he thought. He slipped out of bed, tiptoed across to the window and opened the curtains just a little.

He could just about make out Odds-and-Ends in the darkness. Every now and then,

the little dragon flew by as he patrolled
the garden. Freddy slipped back into bed.

He felt happy knowing he had a house dragon to protect him from Dragon Ormudd. He still couldn't get to sleep, though. As he lay in the darkness, he remembered something he had seen when he was looking for a book on flying spells. He leapt out of bed, lit a candle and tiptoed downstairs. In the wizard room, he held the candle up to the shelves while he ran his finger along the books.

"Ah! This is what I'm looking for!" he said. "I knew I had seen this before." He pulled out a book called *All You Need to Know About Dragons.*

He laid the candle on the table and began to flick through the pages. He found what he was looking for in the chapter called *House Dragons.*

House dragons are small and only kept by wizards. They have no magic powers but can sometimes protect the house from danger by flying round the outside walls.

"Danger!" whispered Freddy nervously.

He looked down at the book again. The chapter after the one called *House Dragons* was called *Dangerous Dragons*. He flicked through the pages until he found it:

Dragon Ormudd.

A cold shiver ran down his spine as he read:

Dragon Ormudd – A very dangerous and unpleasant dragon. Moves from country to country, hiding in damp caves. Can drink whole rivers dry and burn oak trees to ash. Searches out wizards' potions, which he likes to eat. Can smell a wizard's house from a great distance.

Freddy slammed the book shut and ran back upstairs. He sat down nervously on the edge of the bed.

"Dragon Ormudd might be dangerous but I'm sure Odds will keep Wizard Cottage safe," he said to himself. "Odds could knock the spots off any dragon!"

He pulled the lever on the speaking clock yet again.

"*The time is sixteen minutes past one in the morning. The weather is hot and cloudy.*"

"Hot and cloudy?" cried Freddy. "How could it have changed from cool and clear so quickly?" Then he realised why – smoke and fire from a dragon's breath would turn cool and clear into hot and cloudy. At that moment Wizard Cottage began to shake. There was a roar like thunder outside. Dragon Ormudd had arrived.

Freddy dived towards the window. Another cold shiver ran from the top of his head down to his little toes and back again.

Why did I think Odds could deal with Dragon Ormudd? thought Freddy in panic. I never thought Ormudd would be the size... of a house!

The huge dragon hovered in the air near Wizard Cottage. His growling rattled the glass in the windows. Just then, something shot towards Ormudd with

great speed
and hit him
on the nose.
It was Odds-
and-Ends. For a
moment Dragon
Ormudd looked
surprised. He took
a swipe with his huge
claws, but Odds-and-Ends
was too nimble for him. The
little dragon flew around the big
one, tweaking his ears and pulling at
his scales.

Freddy jumped up and down at the

window, shouting, "That's it Odds! Go
for it Odds! Show him what you can do!"

Then, with one flick of a huge paw, Dragon Ormudd caught Odds-and-Ends.

"Oh no!" squeaked Freddy. He turned and ran downstairs. He burst out of the front door and sped across the grass, waving his arms wildly.

"Put him down!" he yelled. "Leave him alone you great, ugly, smelly *pimple*!"

Dragon Ormudd opened his mouth wide to show rows of spiky teeth, but he didn't gobble up Odds-and-Ends. Instead, he gave a long, noisy yawn. Then, with one flap of his enormous wings, he rose into the sky, still clutching Odds-and-Ends. As he disappeared into the darkness, he looked over his shoulder. Freddy was sure he saw an "I'll be back" look in his eyes.

chapter Five

Freddy threw himself down on the garden seat. He sat there for a long time, wondering how he could rescue Odds-and-Ends. As it began to get light he saw the mess which Dragon Ormudd had left

behind. The fence, gate and bushes were flattened and there were scorch marks on the grass.

In fact, there was a trail of scorch marks starting at the garden gate and disappearing into the distance.

In the book about dragons, it said that Ormudd liked hiding in damp caves, Freddy thought. *The only caves around here are in the Tusker Mountains. I bet if I followed the scorch marks they would lead me to the caves and I could rescue Odds. But the caves are far away – it would take ages to reach them.*

Then he had a clever thought. *It would be quicker if I* flew *there. If a birthday cake can fly, then so can I!*

He dashed into the wizard room, found his wand and pointed it at himself.

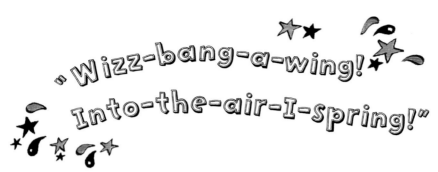

"Wizz-bang-a-wing!
Into-the-air-I-spring!"

Instantly, Freddy had a pair of wings on his back. He gave them a little flap and his feet left the floor.

"Wow!" he cried. "Odds, here I come!"

And he took to the air.

But flying wasn't as easy as Freddy thought, especially as he seemed to have one wing as big as an eagle's and the other as small as a sparrow's.

"Ouch!" he cried, as he missed the door and crashed against the wall. Once

he was outside, he got the hang of flying, though the journey was a slow one. He fell into the river twice and got soaked. He dropped into Widow Wainscott's chicken coop and sent the hens screeching in all directions.

He dive-bombed Mr Mullygrump on his cart. Lily, the old horse pulling the cart, ran off in panic and Mullygrump had to hang on for dear life to stop himself falling off.

Before he reached the Tusker Mountains, Freddy had to untangle himself from three washing lines and a very prickly holly bush.

No one came to the Tusker Mountains unless they had to. It was a damp, misty and unfriendly place. Freddy flew slowly along, calling out "Odds? Are you there, Odds?" His voice echoed back from the rocks: "odds? odds? odds?"

Then he heard a deep growling sound, and he knew he was near Dragon Ormudd's den. As he came round a big rock he saw a wisp of smoke drifting out from the mouth of a cave. Freddy put his hand nervously on his wand and flew towards it.

He peered in and when his eyes got used to the dark he saw a huge creature coiled up just inside. It was Dragon Ormudd.

chapter six

"Master Freddy!" called a little voice. Freddy looked up and saw Odds-and-Ends trapped in a cage made of stones high on the cave wall.

"Master Freddy! You should not be

here!" squeaked the little dragon. "It is terribly dangerous!"

"I've come to get you out," said Freddy, as he flew up to the cage. He was able to lift a stone on top of the cage, just enough for Odds-and-Ends to squeeze out.

"Why didn't Dragon Ormudd come back to raid Wizard Cottage after he had caught you?" Freddy asked.

"Just look at him!" said Odds-and-Ends. "He's fat and unfit and needed a rest. That's what happens when you gobble up too many magic potions! But come on, we must leave quickly before he wakes! Perhaps he'll be too puffed out to follow us."

But Odds-and-Ends was wrong. As they reached Wizard Cottage they felt Dragon Ormudd's hot breath on their backs. At that moment, Freddy's flying spell ran out, his wings vanished and he tumbled on to the grass.

As he stood up, he saw Dragon Ormudd diving towards him. The creature had a mean look in his eyes, but before he could pounce, Odds-and-Ends hurled himself forwards and hit the big dragon on the nose.

Odds-and-Ends darted off and Dragon Ormudd went after him.

Freddy leapt to his feet and pulled his wand from his belt. He had come up with a plan that might stop Dragon Ormudd.

"Odds! Head for the net!" he yelled. **"HEAD FOR THE NET!"**

The little dragon saw what his master meant. Down by the river stood two trees. These were Freddy's goalposts and a big net was stretched between them. Odds-and-Ends flew like the wind towards the goal net.

With perfect timing, Freddy cast his spell.

"Wizzbang-a-thingummyjig! Stretch-stretch-really big!"

Suddenly, the net stretched so that Odds-and-Ends flew quite easily through one of the holes. Dragon Ormudd was much bigger, and before he could stop, he flew slap-bang into the net. There was a ripping noise as the net came away from the trees and Dragon Ormudd tumbled down, tangled in fishing net.

"Wizzbang-I-call! Net-shrink-small!"

Freddy yelled.

Dragon Ormudd let out a roar as the net tightened around him. To his dismay, Freddy saw that the net was not going to hold the big, struggling dragon for long.

Just then, a dark cloud appeared over Dragon Ormudd's head. The dragon had knocked over Mr Buzzwell's beehive with his thrashing tail, and a cloud of angry bees was on the warpath.

"Let's see if this will work," said Freddy, as he twirled his magic wand again.

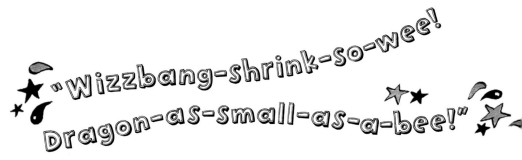

"Wizzbang-shrink-so-wee!
Dragon-as-small-as-a-bee!"

Ormudd began to shrink and shrink.

At last a tiny dragon no bigger

than a bee flew out of the

tangled net and shot

off, chased by

the angry

swarm.

That evening, Freddy sat on the seat outside the door of Wizard Cottage. He was feeling pleased with himself. He had used magic to deal with a very nasty dragon, even if it wasn't the kind of proper magic his Great Uncle Sneezer would have used.

Odds-and-Ends came flying round the end of the cottage. "Master Freddy, I am sorry I have been bad-tempered these last few days, but I knew Dragon Ormudd was around and it was my duty to protect Wizard Cottage."

"And you did. Thanks very much,

Odds," said Freddy. "You were very brave. I had no idea that Ormudd was so big. I suppose he'll return to his normal size and might come back sometime?"

"Perhaps, but not for a very long time," said Odds-and-Ends. "Now, if you were a good student you would have found out how to deal with him in the *Wizard's Handbook*, but—"

"Odds," said Freddy, putting his hand on the wand in his belt. "Would you like to be half the size you are now?"

"Oh, Master Freddy!" squeaked the little dragon, and he flew away quickly round the end of the cottage.

Sainsbury's
Reading Scheme

CERTIFICATE
of Reading

My name is

_____

I have read

_____

Date

_____